HOUGHTON

SOCIAL STUDIES

TENNESSEE

TCAP Test Practice and Assessment Options

....

★ **Unit and Chapter Assessments**

★ **Test Practice in TCAP Format**
- Aligned with Tennessee Social Studies SPI's
- Full-Length TCAP Practice Test

Visit *Education Place*
www.eduplace.com/kids

HOUGHTON MIFFLIN   BOSTON

MANY REGIONS, ONE WORLD

Credits
Illustrations: © Houghton Mifflin School Division
Maps: Mapping Specialists, Ltd.

Printed in the U.S.A.

ISBN 10: 0-618-93818-4
ISBN 13: 978-0-618-93818-6

1 2 3 4 5 6 7 8 9 POO 16 15 14 13 12 11 10 09 08

HOUGHTON MIFFLIN
SOCIAL STUDIES

Contents

Assessment Options

Contents

TCAP Test Practice

Chapter 1 Test

Test Your Knowledge

ethnic group	region	culture

Fill in the blank with the correct word from the box.

1 Italians are a large ___ethnic group___ in the United States. 3.1.01b, 3.1.spi.1

2 A(n) ___region___ is an area that shares one or more features. 3.3.03c, 3.3.spi.1

3 The food you eat and the clothing you wear are parts of your ___culture___. 3.1.01b, 3.1.spi.1

Circle the letter of the best answer.

4 What is one way that all cultures are alike? 3.1.02a, 3.1.spi.1

Ⓐ They all have the same language.

Ⓑ They all have the same basic needs.

Ⓒ They all have the same laws and rules.

Ⓓ They all have the same ways of worship.

5 This picture shows how some people meet their need for 3.1.02a, 3.1.spi.2

Ⓐ food.

Ⓑ shelter.

Ⓒ clothing.

Ⓓ communication.

Name _____ Date _____

Test the Skill: Review Map Skills

The State of Tennessee

Kentucky

★ Nashville

TENNESSEE

• Memphis

X

Georgia

Alabama

Map Key
• City
★ Capital
— Border

0   miles   100

NW N NE / W E / SW S SE

6 What is the title of this map?

The State of Tennessee
3.3.01a

7 In what direction would a person driving from Nashville to Memphis be traveling?

southwest
3.3.01c, 3.3.spi.6

8 Who might take care of a road that leads from Nashville to Memphis?

the state government of Tennessee
3.3.01a, 3.3.spi.2

Apply the Skill

9 Now give directions from the X on the border of Georgia to Nashville. Give the direction a person should go and tell about how many miles it is.

Sample answer: The person should go northwest from the X.

It is about 150 miles.
3.3.01c, 3.3.spi.4

Chapter 2 Test

Test Your Knowledge

| custom | honor | heritage |

Fill in the blank with the correct word from the box.

1 In Moscow, it is the _____ custom _____ to have school recess inside. 3.1.01b

2 On Memorial Day, we _____ honor _____ people who lost their lives in war. 3.1.03b

3 The history, ideas, and beliefs people receive from the past is their _____ heritage _____. 3.1.02c

Circle the letter of the best answer.

4 In what way do Jews celebrate Rosh Ha-Shanah?
3.1.03a, 3.1.spi:1
Ⓐ Jews ring church bells in the evening.
Ⓑ Jews fast from sunrise to sunset each day.
Ⓒ Jewish families share a special meal at home.
Ⓓ Jewish adults give children money in red envelopes.

5 What tradition does Patricia McKissack believe in?
3.1.02c
Ⓐ creating art
Ⓑ telling stories
Ⓒ making pottery
Ⓓ painting pictures

Test the Skill: Give a Speech

> **Topics for Giving a Speech:**
> - Aaron Douglas
> - Patricia McKissack

6 After choosing one of the topics listed above, what would be the next step in preparing your speech?

Sample answer: I would need to find more information on my topic.
PS.3a

7 What questions would you ask in order to find the information you need about your topic?

Sample answer: Where was the person born? What are some of the

person's best-known works? What were important life events of the

person? How is the person important to Tennessee culture?
PS.2a

8 In what way could you prepare yourself for giving your speech? What would you need?

Sample answer: Note cards are helpful in preparing a speech.

Also, I would need to practice giving the speech before I present it.
PS.3a

Apply the Skill

9 Pretend you are going to give a speech to your class about Cultural Traditions of Tennessee. Describe each step that you would take before presenting your speech to the class.

Sample answer: I would first research by asking questions like:

What kind of traditions are there in Tennessee? Where are they

from? Who celebrates them and why? Then I would write the

speech based on what I find. I would use note cards and practice

my speech before presenting to the class.
PS.2a

Name _____ Date _____

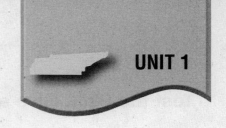

Unit Performance Assessment

Make an Oral Presentation

You have been learning about cultural and religious holidays celebrated in the United States. Holidays are times to celebrate special events or people.

> Use what you have learned in this unit to describe two holidays many Americans celebrate.
>
> Prepare and make an oral presentation to your class that describes one cultural holiday and one religious holiday.
>
> Explain when, why, and how each holiday is celebrated. Put your information on note cards in the order you will present it. Then make two drawings, one for each holiday. Use both your notes and drawings to support your presentation. Plan an interesting way to begin and end your presentation. Include the important facts in the middle.

Use this checklist to help you plan the presentation:

☐ **1.** My presentation describes a cultural holiday and explains when, why, and how it is celebrated. I have made a drawing that supports these details.

☐ **2.** My presentation describes a religious holiday and explains when, why, and how it is celebrated. I have made a drawing that supports these details.

☐ **3.** My presentation is organized in an order that makes sense. It has a beginning, a middle, and an end.

3.1.03a, PS.3a

Help Students Prepare for the Unit Performance Assessment

- Students will work independently. Remind them to use what they have learned in the unit, as specific information will improve their scores. Tell students their scores will be based on the points in the checklist.

- Discuss what makes a good presentation, such as speaking clearly and presenting information in an order that makes sense.

- You may wish to suggest students use a Venn diagram to compare and contrast their holidays.

	Unit Performance Assessment Rubric
4	• Presentation clearly and accurately describes a cultural holiday and tells how, why, and when it is celebrated. A drawing supports the details. • Presentation clearly and accurately describes a religious holiday and tells how, why, and when it is celebrated. A drawing supports the details. • Presentation is organized in a clear, logical order.
3	• Presentation adequately describes a cultural holiday and tells how, why, and when it is celebrated. A drawing supports some details. • Presentation adequately describes a religious holiday and tells how, why, and when it is celebrated. A drawing supports some details. • Presentation generally follows a logical order.
2	• Presentation describes a cultural holiday but may include only one or two facts about it. Drawing is general and does not support the details. • Presentation describes a religious holiday but may include only one or two facts about it. Drawing is general and does not support the details. • Presentation has a loose organizational structure. Some explanations or descriptions are repeated.
1	• Presentation names a cultural holiday but does not tell how, why, or when it is celebrated. No drawing is included. • Presentation names a religious holiday but does not tell how, why, or when it is celebrated. No drawing is included. • Presentation has little, if any, organizational structure. The lack of organization affects meaning.

Chapter 3 Test

Test Your Knowledge

| climate | continent | natural resources |

Write *T* if the statement is true or *F* if it is false.

1 ___T___ The weather of a place over a long time is called the climate. 3.3.02b, 3.3.spi.5

2 ___F___ The United States is a continent. 3.3.02b, 3.3.spi.1

3 ___T___ Natural resources are things from nature that people use. 3.6.01b, 3.6.spi.3

Circle the letter of the best answer.

4 **What is geography?**
3.3.02d, 3.3.spi.9
Ⓐ It is the study of time and place.
Ⓑ It is the study of animals and zoos.
Ⓒ It is the study of people and places.
Ⓓ It is the study of weather and nature.

5 **Why do people live near rivers?**
3.3.02b, 3.3.spi.5
Ⓐ People use them for erosion.
Ⓑ People fish for saltwater fish.
Ⓒ People use them to travel up mountains.
Ⓓ People use them for fresh water to drink.

Name _____ Date _____

Test the Skill: Read a Climate Map

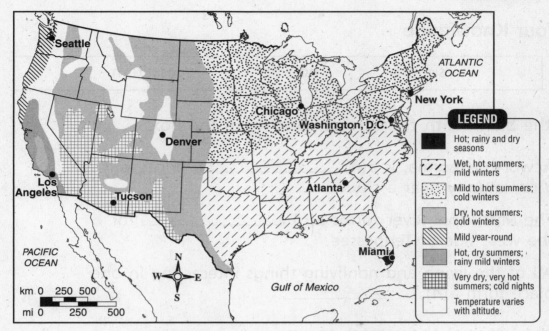

LEGEND

■ Hot; rainy and dry seasons

▨ Wet, hot summers; mild winters

▨ Mild to hot summers; cold winters

▨ Dry, hot summers; cold winters

▨ Mild year-round

▨ Hot, dry summers; rainy mild winters

▨ Very dry, very hot summers; cold nights

□ Temperature varies with altitude.

6 Look at the map. What is the climate like in Chicago?

mild to hot summers; cold winters

3.3.02b, 3.3.spi.7

7 Name a city with wet, hot summers and mild winters.

Atlanta

3.3.02b, 3.3.spi.7

8 Which city gets more rain, Tucson or Miami?

Miami

3.3.02b, 3.3.spi.7

Apply the Skill

9 If someone wanted to live in a place where it never got too hot or too cold, in what city do you think they could live? Why?

Sample answer: Seattle is mild year-round.

3.3.02b, 3.3.spi.7

Chapter 4 Test

Test Your Knowledge

suburb	border	ecosystem

Fill in the blank with the correct word from the box.

1 Acworth, Georgia, is a(n) _____suburb_____ because it is a community near a city. 3.3.03f

2 The Mississippi River forms a(n) _____border_____ for the west side of Tennessee. 3.3.02b, 3.3.spi.9

3 All of the living and nonliving things interacting in one place form a(n)_____ecosystem_____. 3.3.02c, 3.3.spi.8

Circle the letter of the correct answer.

4 What is a rural community? 3.3.03f
  Ⓐ It is a community with many offices and shops.
  Ⓑ It is a large city with many people and buildings.
  Ⓒ It is a community near a city, but not as crowded.
  Ⓓ It is a small community surrounded by farms or open land.

5 How is Tokyo, Japan, different from Memphis, Tennessee? 3.3.02a
  Ⓐ It has factories.
  Ⓑ It has transportation.
  Ⓒ It has suburbs nearby.
  Ⓓ It has a greater population.

Name _____ Date _____

Test the Skill: Use Longitude and Latitude

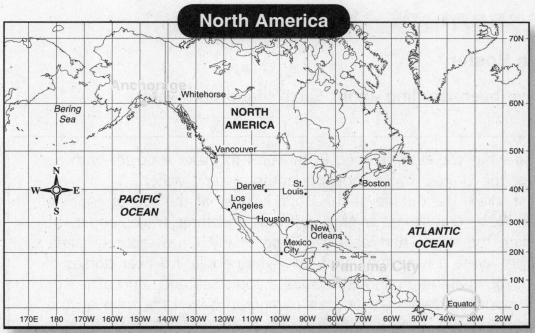

6 Which city is nearest to 70° west longitude?

Boston

3.3.01a

7 Circle the name for 0° latitude.

3.3.01a

8 Through which two cities does 90° west longitude pass?

St. Louis and New Orleans

3.3.01a

Apply the Skill

9 Add two more labels to the map. Use the locations below. Write the names of the cities on the map.

Anchorage: 60°N, 150°W

Panama City: 10°N, 80°W

Name _____ Date _____

Unit Performance Assessment

Make a Poster

You have been learning about Earth's land and water.

Use what you have learned in this unit to make a poster with a map of the United States showing landforms and water.

First, draw the outline of the United States at the top of your poster. Next, draw three major landforms and three major bodies of water on the map. Then label each one clearly. On a separate sheet of paper, write a paragraph that tells why people live near bodies of water. Your paragraph should include a topic sentence and at least two supporting details. Paste your paragraph below the map on the poster.

Use this checklist to help you make the poster:

☐ **1.** My poster shows and labels three different major landforms on a map of the United States.

☐ **2.** My poster shows and labels my map with three different major bodies of water in the United States or bordering it.

☐ **3.** My paragraph explains why people live near bodies of water. It includes a clear topic sentence and at least two supporting details.

☐ **4.** I have proofread my paragraph to correct any mistakes in spelling, capitalization, and punctuation.

3.3.02b, 3.3.spi.5, PS.2

Help Students Prepare for the Unit Performance Assessment

- Students will work independently. Remind them to use what they have learned in the unit, as specific information will improve their scores. Tell students their scores will be based on the points in the checklist.
- Write a topic sentence on the board. Have students suggest supporting details or examples.
- Review rules for spelling, capitalization, and punctuation. Remind students to proofread their paragraphs carefully.

Unit Performance Assessment Rubric	
4	• Map on poster accurately shows and labels three major landforms in the United States. • Map on poster accurately shows and labels three major bodies of water in or bordering the U.S. • Paragraph clearly and accurately explains why people live near bodies of water. It includes an appropriate topic sentence and two supporting details. • Paragraph has very few or no errors in spelling, capitalization, or punctuation.
3	• Poster accurately shows and labels two major landforms on a map of the United States. • Map on poster accurately shows and labels two major bodies of water in or bordering the U.S. • Paragraph generally explains why people live near bodies of water. It includes a topic sentence and gives at least one supporting detail. • Paragraph has a few errors in spelling, capitalization, or punctuation.
2	• Poster accurately shows and labels one major landform on a map of the United States. • Map on poster accurately shows and labels one major body of water in or bordering the U.S. • Paragraph partially explains why people live near water. There is no clear topic sentence or example. • Paragraph has several errors in spelling, capitalization, or punctuation that affect meaning.
1	• Poster does not have a map of the United States and does not show or label any major landforms. • Poster does not show or label any major bodies of water on a U.S. map. • Paragraph does not explain why people live near water. • Paragraph contains numerous errors in spelling, capitalization, and punctuation that affect meaning.

Chapter 5 Test

Test Your Knowledge

barter	goods	scarcity

Fill in the blank with the correct word from the box.

1 In a _____ economy, people exchange goods
or services for other goods or services.

2 You can buy _____ in a grocery store.

3 When there are not enough goods, there is a
_____ of them.

Circle the letter of the best answer.

4 Why do more people use money than barter?

Ⓐ Money is like barter.

Ⓑ Money helps people make better decisions.

Ⓒ Barter is better than money for buying things.

Ⓓ Money is easy to carry and everyone knows what it is worth.

5 What is a budget?

Ⓐ what banks pay

Ⓑ an exchange of goods

Ⓒ a plan for using money

Ⓓ money that people earn for work

Test the Skill: Identify Cause and Effect

> People must earn money in order to pay for goods and services. They get jobs and earn money, or income. They save some of their income for items such as cars that cost a lot of money.

6 What happens first, the cause or the effect?

cause
3.5.02b, 3.5.spi.3

7 How do people earn money?

They earn money by working jobs that give them income.

3.5.02b, 3.5.spi.3

8 Study the paragraph. What do people do with the money that they don't spend?

People can save it to buy expensive items, such as cars.

3.5.02b, 3.5.spi.3

Apply the Skill

9 Label each sentence. Which is the cause and which is the effect?

A. A man decides he wants to save money.

cause

B. A man puts his money in a bank account.

effect
3.3.02b

Chapter 6 Test

Test Your Knowledge

| producer | capital resources | assembly line |

Write *T* if the statement is true or *F* if it is false.

1 ___T___ A farmer who grows crops is one kind of producer. 3.2.03a

2 ___F___ Capital resources are the skills and hard work of people.
3.2.03f, 3.2.spi.1

3 ___T___ Each worker on an assembly line completes just one step.
3.2.03f, 3.2.spi.1

Circle the letter of the best answer.

4 Importing gives consumers more choices and
3.2.02d, 3.2.spi.3
  Ⓐ gives farmers a vacation.
  Ⓑ gives consumers fewer choices.
  Ⓒ lets them sell goods at a lower cost.
  Ⓓ lets them buy some goods at lower cost.

5 The United States and other nations export goods and services because
3.2.02d, 3.2.spi.3
  Ⓐ they need more goods and services.
  Ⓑ it helps them sell more of these things.
  Ⓒ they do not need any goods and services.
  Ⓓ other countries do not need more goods and services.

Name _____ Date _____

Test the Skill: Use a Flow Chart

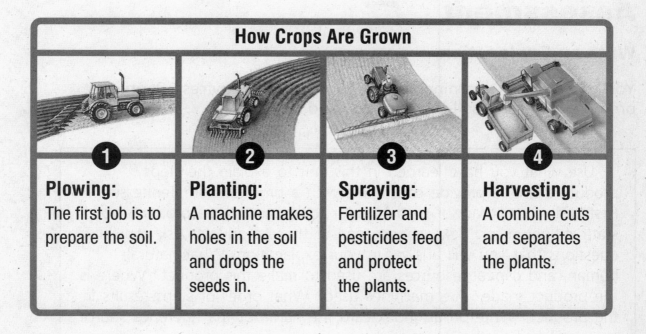

How Crops Are Grown

1 Plowing: The first job is to prepare the soil.

2 Planting: A machine makes holes in the soil and drops the seeds in.

3 Spraying: Fertilizer and pesticides feed and protect the plants.

4 Harvesting: A combine cuts and separates the plants.

6 What is the topic of this flow chart?

growing crops
3.2.03d

7 How many steps are shown in the flow chart?

4
3.2.03d

8 What happens in the second step?

Seeds are planted.
3.2.03d

Apply the Skill

9 Create a simple flow chart to show how you would grow flowers. Draw pictures and write labels and a title. Number the steps.
PS.20

Name _____ Date _____

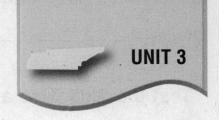

UNIT 3

Unit Performance Assessment

Write an Explanation

You have been learning about goods and services. People produce, buy, and sell many goods and services.

> Use what you have learned in this unit to explain the steps producers use to provide consumers with a product from Tennessee. First, visit your library or media center to research three products your state is known for. Next, choose one of these products. Ask yourself questions that you will answer in your explanation. What natural, human, and capital resources are used to make this product? Where is the product made? Are machines used? What order of steps results in the product? Write on an index card the name of the reference source you used to find the information.
>
> Then write your explanation. Name the product and describe the three kinds of resources used to make it. Explain how the product is made and how it gets to consumers. Write the steps in that order.

Use this checklist to help you write the explanation:

❏ **1.** I have used reference sources to research and choose a product from Tennessee.

❏ **2.** I have identified the resources used to produce the product for consumers.

❏ **3.** My explanation lists in order the steps needed to make the product.

❏ **4.** I have proofread my explanation to correct mistakes in spelling, capitalization, and punctuation. I have listed the name of the reference source I used.

3.2.03I, 3.2.spi.1, PS.1

Help Students Prepare for the Unit Performance Assessment

- Students will work independently. Remind them to use what they have learned in the unit, as specific information will improve their scores. Tell students their scores will be based on the points in the checklist.

- Remind students how to search for information using library or Internet resources. Review correct methods for listing sources.

- Emphasize that the students' products must use Tennessee's resources. Discuss available resources and different types of products.

Unit Performance Assessment Rubric

4	• The product chosen is made in Tennessee as determined by effective research. • Explanation clearly and accurately categorizes and lists natural, human, and capital resources needed to make the product. • Explanation has a complete and accurate sequence of steps. • Explanation has few, if any, mistakes in mechanics. The reference source is listed.
3	• The product chosen is made in Tennessee. Adequate research has been used. • Explanation lists natural, human, and capital resources and most of these resources are classified correctly. • Explanation is organized into a sequence of steps that is accurate but not detailed. • Explanation has a few mistakes in spelling, capitalization, or punctuation, but they do not affect meaning. The reference source is listed.
2	• The product chosen is made in Tennessee. Research has been attempted but may be incomplete. • Explanation lists most of the resources needed but may incorrectly classify them. • Explanation is written in steps, but steps may be out of order or incomplete. • Explanation has some mistakes in spelling, capitalization, or punctuation that affect meaning. A resource is listed but may not have complete information.
1	• The product chosen either is not made in Tennessee or may be a resource rather than a product. Research has been minimally attempted. • Explanation is incomplete. Resources used in making the product are inaccurate or missing. • Writing does not give steps for making the product but focuses on some other aspect of the product. • Writing has many mistakes in spelling, capitalization, or punctuation that affect meaning. No reference source is listed.

Chapter 7 Test

Test Your Knowledge

volunteer	responsibility	vote

Fill in the blank with the correct word from the box.

1 When you _____vote_____ you make an official choice. 3.4.03e

2 A duty you should do is a ____responsibility____. 3.4.03e

3 A ____volunteer____ is someone who works without pay. 3.4.03g

Circle the letter of the best answer.

4 How might citizens improve their community? 3.4.03g, 3.4.spi.2

Ⓐ They might watch movies.

Ⓑ They might read more magazines.

Ⓒ They might throw trash on the street.

Ⓓ They might work together to clean up a park.

5 What does it mean to work for the common good? 3.4.03g, 3.4.spi.2

Ⓐ People solve their own problems without help.

Ⓑ People make sure they stay as busy as possible.

Ⓒ People stay home and do not take part in the community.

Ⓓ People do whatever helps the most people in their community.

Test the Skill: Point of View

The small community of Westville was electing a mayor. There were three candidates, or people who wanted the job. They were Mrs. Black, Mr. White, and Miss Brown. Before the election, Westville held a town meeting. Citizens asked the candidates questions. Each candidate had a different idea about what Westville needed most. Here are their points of view.

Mrs. Black: "I think we need to improve our bus service. We need at least two more buses and more bus stops."
Mr. White: "Westville has too much litter. The first thing I would do is pass more laws about littering."
Miss Brown: "Westville is growing. Our fire department needs to grow, too. We need three more firefighters."

6 Whose points of view do citizens want to learn about?
the candidates
3.4.03a

7 Summarize Mr. White's point of view.
Sample answer: The community needs more laws against littering.

_____
3.4.03a

8 Which two people have points of view about city services?
Mrs. Black and Miss Brown
3.4.03a

Apply the Skill

9 If this election was in your community, which point of view would you agree with the most? Why?
Answers will vary.

_____

_____

_____
3.4.03a

Chapter 8 Test

Test Your Knowledge

tax	judicial branch	public policy

Write *T* if the statement is true or *F* if it is false.

1 ___T___ A local government might collect a tax to pay for schools. 3.4.02a

2 ___T___ The judicial branch of the national government decides what the laws mean. 3.4.03b

3 ___T___ Public policy is the government's plan for solving problems or giving people services. 3.4.03d

Circle the letter of the best answer.

4 What does a governor do?
3.4.01a
   Ⓐ breaks the laws
   Ⓑ carries out laws
   Ⓒ makes new laws
   Ⓓ questions the laws

5 Where do leaders make the laws?
3.4.01b
   Ⓐ in schools
   Ⓑ in churches
   Ⓒ at the library
   Ⓓ at the capital

Test the Skill: Read a Map Scale

The Ohio River

6 What does the map scale show?

distance in kilometers and miles

3.3.01a

7 About how far is it from St. Louis to Baltimore on the National Road?

950 km or 600 mi

3.3.01a

8 About how far would you travel if you went from Boston to New York City and back to Boston?

700 km or 400 mi

3.3.01a

Apply the Skill

9 Why is the distance people have to travel to get somewhere often longer than the actual distance between two places?

Highways might have to go around geographical blockages.

_____

_____

_____

3.3.01a

Name _____ Date _____

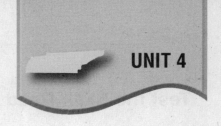

Unit Performance Assessment

Plan and Give a Speech

You have been learning about being a citizen in the United States. American citizens have both rights and responsibilities.

> Use what you have learned in this unit to write and present a speech to your class about Americans' rights and responsibilities.
> First, explain the meanings of the words right and responsibility. Then name two rights of U.S. citizens and two responsibilities of U.S. citizens. Last, draw a conclusion about how these rights and responsibilities affect citizens. Make sure your speech has a clear beginning, middle, and end.

Use this checklist to help you prepare the speech:

❏ **1.** My speech explains what a right is and describes two rights of U.S. citizens.

❏ **2.** My speech explains what a responsibility is and describes two responsibilities of U.S. citizens.

❏ **3.** My speech draws a conclusion about how these rights and responsibilities affect citizens.

❏ **4.** My speech has a clear beginning, middle, and end.
  3.4.03c, PS.3

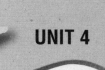
Help Students Prepare for the Unit Performance Assessment

- Students will work independently. Remind them to use what they have learned in the unit, as specific information will improve their scores. Tell students their scores will be based on the points in the checklist.

- Have students name some rights and responsibilities of citizens.

- Discuss different ways to begin a speech, such as with a question or an interesting fact. Remind students that the ending of a speech may sum up the most important information or give an opinion.

- Also remind students to speak clearly and to look at their audience when they give their speech.

	Unit Performance Assessment Rubric
4	• Speech accurately defines the word right and describes two rights of U.S. citizens. • Speech accurately defines the word responsibility and describes two responsibilities of U.S. citizens. • Speech draws a logical conclusion on the effect of rights and responsibilities on citizens. • Speech has an effective beginning, middle, and end.
3	• Speech adequately defines the word right and describes one or two rights of U.S. citizens. • Speech adequately defines the word responsibility and describes one or two responsibilities of U.S. citizens. • Speech draws a plausible conclusion on the effect of rights and responsibilities on citizens. • Speech has a clear beginning and middle but may lack a clear ending.
2	• Speech mentions only one right of U.S. citizens and does not clearly define right. • Speech mentions only one responsibility of U.S. citizens and does not clearly define responsibility. • Speech tells an effect of rights and responsibilities on citizens but does not draw a conclusion. • Speech lacks a clear beginning or end
1	• Speech does not show an understanding of rights of U.S. citizens and does not define right. • Speech does not show an understanding of responsibilities of U.S. citizens or define the term. • Speech does not draw a conclusion. • Speech has little or no organization.

25

Name _____ Date _____

Chapter 9 Test

Test Your Knowledge

treaty	justice	civil rights

Fill in the blank with the correct word from the box.

1 The Cherokee and the settlers were working on an agreement called a _____treaty_____. 3.5.01a

2 Abraham Lincoln believed in _____justice_____ for enslaved people. 3.5.01b

3 Dr. Martin Luther King, Jr., fought for the _____civil rights_____ of all people. 3.5.01b

Circle the letter of the best answer.

4 What did the suffragists do? 3.5.03b
  Ⓐ They hired African Americans.
  Ⓑ They created the United Nations.
  Ⓒ They built new roads and schools.
  Ⓓ They worked for women's right to vote.

5 In what way did Cesar Chavez help our country? 3.5.03b
  Ⓐ He helped free many slaves.
  Ⓑ He worked for women's rights.
  Ⓒ He spoke out for farm workers.
  Ⓓ He led the country's fight for freedom.

Name _____ Date _____

Test the Skill: Read and Interpret a Timeline

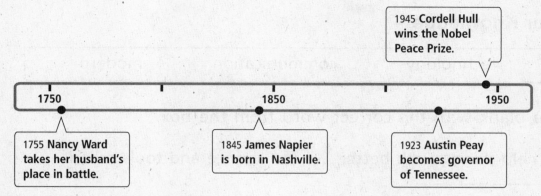

1945 Cordell Hull wins the Nobel Peace Prize.

1750   1850   1950

1755 Nancy Ward takes her husband's place in battle.

1845 James Napier is born in Nashville.

1923 Austin Peay becomes governor of Tennessee.

6 In what year does the first decade of this timeline start?

1750

3.5.03a, 3.5.spi.2

7 Who won a major prize one hundred years after James Napier was born?

Cordell Hull

3.5.03a, 3.5.spi.2

8 Who became governor more than 150 years after Nancy Ward went into battle?

Austin Peay

3.5.03a, 3.5.spi.2

Apply the Skill

9 Use the line below to create a timeline. Begin with the year 1780. End it with 1900. The lines show every 20 years. Label the missing years. Then fill in the dates and events below. You may shorten the event labels.

1789; George Washington becomes first President.
1820; Susan B. Anthony born.
1863; Abraham Lincoln announces freedom for southern slaves.

3.4.03a

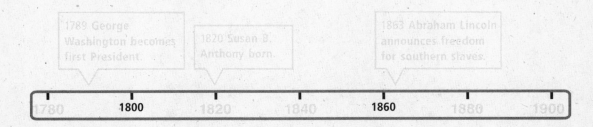

1789 George Washington becomes first President.

1820 Susan B. Anthony born.

1863 Abraham Lincoln announces freedom for southern slaves.

1780   1800   1820   1840   1860   1880   1900

Chapter 10 Test

Test Your Knowledge

technology	communication	modern

Fill in the blank with the correct word from the box.

1 To help things work better, we use science and tools called _____. 3.5.02b

2 People exchange information through _____. 3.5.02b

3 Today, Athens is a _____ city in the country of Greece. 3.5.02a

Circle the letter of the best answer.

4 How do artifacts help people?
3.5.02c, 3.5.spi.1
Ⓐ They help people study the future.
Ⓑ They help people use transportation.
Ⓒ They help people understand the past.
Ⓓ They help people learn to communicate.

5 When did the Olympics start in Athens?
3.5.02c, 3.5.spi.1
Ⓐ in the past
Ⓑ in the future
Ⓒ at the present time
Ⓓ during modern times

Name _____ Date _____

Test the Skill: Primary and Secondary Sources

Chattanooga has changed over the years. In the 1800s, the Chattanooga Railroad connected the city to other parts of the country. Today, cars have replaced trains as Chattanooga's major form of transportation.

6 What is the subject of the source above?

Transportation in Chattanooga

3.1.02b

7 Is this a primary or a secondary source? How can you tell?

secondary; it describes a broad time period

3.1.02b

8 How can you tell that a piece of writing is a primary source?

uses "I, we, or me"

3.1.02b

Apply the Skill

9 Write two sentences as examples of the type of sentence you might expect to find in a primary source about moving to Chattanooga in the 1860s.

Sample answer: I was scared to move to a new place. I could only

bring along a few things.

_____

_____

_____

3.1.02b

Unit Performance Assessment

Write a Letter

You have been learning about the city of Chattanooga in the 1800s. Because Chattanooga was near the railroad, it grew quickly into a big city.

> Use what you have learned in this unit to write a letter that a young person living in Chattanooga in the middle 1800s might have written to a friend in Boston.
>
> In your letter, tell how your family makes a living. Give specific details about the kinds of businesses started in Chattanooga. Give specific details about transportation used to travel to and from Chattanooga. Explain how new technology changed Chattanooga.

Use this checklist to help you prepare the letter:

☐ **1.** My letter gives specific details about how the writer's family earns a living in Chattanooga and about the kinds of businesses there.

☐ **2.** My letter gives specific details about transportation used to travel to and from Chattanooga during the 1800s.

☐ **3.** My letter explains how new technology changed Chattanooga in the 1800s.

☐ **4.** My letter is written in correct friendly-letter form. I have proofread my letter to correct any mistakes in spelling, capitalization, and punctuation.

3.5.03b, PS.4a

Name _____ Date _____

Help Students Prepare for the Unit Performance Assessment

- Students will work independently. Remind them to use what they have learned in the unit, as specific information will improve their scores. Tell students their scores will be based on the points in the checklist.
- Review the parts of a friendly letter.
- Have students name the three main ideas about Chattanooga that they should include in their letter: businesses, transportation, and location. Suggest that they write specific details about each idea in a separate paragraph.

	Unit Performance Assessment Rubric
4	• Letter reflects a strong understanding of the information in the unit. It names a realistic occupation for the period. • Letter clearly and correctly gives specific details about businesses in Chattanooga and transportation to and from there in the 1800s. • Letter effectively explains how new technology changed Chattanooga. • Letter has correct friendly-letter form with very few or no errors in spelling, capitalization, or punctuation.
3	• Letter reflects an adequate understanding of the information in the unit. A reasonable occupation for the period is named. • Letter adequately gives specific details about businesses in Chattanooga and transportation to and from there in the 1800s. • Letter correctly explains how new technology changed Chattanooga. • Letter has correct friendly-letter form with a few errors in spelling, capitalization, or punctuation. The errors do not affect meaning.
2	• Letter reflects a somewhat vague understanding of the information in the unit. An unlikely occupation for the time is mentioned. • Letter gives some specific, but also some incomplete or inaccurate details about businesses and transportation in Chattanooga. • Letter attempts an explanation of how new technology changed Chattanooga. • Letter has incomplete friendly-letter form with several spelling, capitalization, or punctuation errors that affect meaning.
1	• Letter shows a lack of understanding of information in this unit. No occupation is named. • Letter does not describe businesses or methods of transportation to or from Chattanooga. • Letter does not explain how new technology changed Chattanooga. • Letter is missing several parts of a friendly-letter form and has many spelling, capitalization, or punctuation errors that affect meaning.

Assessment Options

Use with *Many Regions, One World*

Multiple-choice Questions

Multiple-choice questions give you different answers to choose from. You must choose the best answer from the choices you are given. These two pages will help you learn to answer multiple-choice questions.

Read the passage and strategies on this page. Then look at the questions on the next page.

How Communities Celebrate

People celebrate holidays for many reasons. People in the United States celebrate many different cultural and religious holidays. People can learn about different ways of life from cultural holidays. For example, Cinco de Mayo is a cultural celebration that honors a battle in Mexican history. Cinco de Mayo means "Fifth of May." Many Mexican Americans celebrate Cinco de Mayo with parades, speeches, and celebrations that include food, music, and dancing.

Another popular cultural holiday is St. Patrick's Day. It is celebrated on March 17th and honors the man who brought Christianity to Ireland. Many cities hold large parades to celebrate this holiday.

People think about their religious beliefs during religious holidays. Some people have special meals. For example, Rosh Ha-Shanah is the Jewish New Year. During Rosh Ha-Shanah, Jews think about the past year. They look ahead to the new year.

1 Find
The main idea of a paragraph is often written in the first sentence.

2 Recognize
Look for helpful details that support the main idea of the passage.

3 Summarize
Think about what you have read. Put the main ideas together in one or two sentences.

S1 What kind of holiday is Rosh Ha-Shanah?
3.1.spi.1

Ⓐ cultural holiday

Ⓑ national holiday

Ⓒ patriotic holiday

Ⓓ religious holiday

Tip
Look for details from the passage.

S2 Cinco de Mayo honors a battle in what country?
3.1.spi.1

Ⓐ China

Ⓑ Ireland

Ⓒ Mexico

Ⓓ United States

Tip
If you are not sure of the answer, reread the passage.

Directions
Use the passage below and what you know to do Numbers 1–3.

Culture in a Community

Culture is a way of life of people in a community. It includes their ideas, language, religion, and history. Children learn about culture from their families, their communities, and even from legends. Legends are stories passed down from one family or group to another over many years. These stories tell about ideas or values that are important in a culture.

All cultures are alike in some ways. All people communicate and need shelter. The language they speak and the clothes they wear may be different in different cultures. For example, in hot dry countries such as Egypt, people wear light clothes that will keep them cool. In cold areas like Norway, people wear heavy clothing to keep them warm.

People from many cultures live in the United States. Some follow the traditions of their <u>ethnic group</u>. An ethnic group is a group of people who have their own language and culture. Americans listen to music from Brazil and play games from Japan.

Legends and folktales show what is important to a culture. In the United States, a well-known folktale tells the story of a man called Johnny Appleseed. He traveled around the country and planted apple seeds. The story of Johnny Appleseed teaches about kindness and the importance of sharing. These are important values in American culture.

Name _____ Date _____

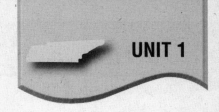

Reporting Category:	3 Human Geography
Performance Indicator:	3.1.spi.2 Determine the similarities and differences in the ways different cultural groups address basic human needs (i.e., food, water, clothing, and shelter by interpreting pictures).

1 Which sentence tells how all cultures are <u>alike</u> in some ways?

Ⓐ Many Americans play games from Japan.

Ⓑ All people communicate and need shelter.

Ⓒ People from many cultures live in the United States.

Ⓓ Some people follow the traditions of their ethnic group.

2 How do people living in Norway deal with cold weather?

Ⓐ by telling legends

Ⓑ by staying indoors

Ⓒ by wearing light clothes

Ⓓ by wearing heavy clothes

3 Why are legends an important part of culture?

Ⓐ They tell how to build houses.

Ⓑ They tell about ideas and values.

Ⓒ They tell how schools teach customs.

Ⓓ They tell how foods are prepared in every culture.

Tip

Read each question carefully. Then go back and answer.

Maps and Graphs

You will find maps, graphs, and other visuals on tests. These contain important information. The reading skills you have learned will help you.

Study the map and strategies on this page. Then look at the questions on the next page.

❶ Identify

Read the title to find out what the map shows.

❷ Recognize

Read the map's labels to find out what is represented.

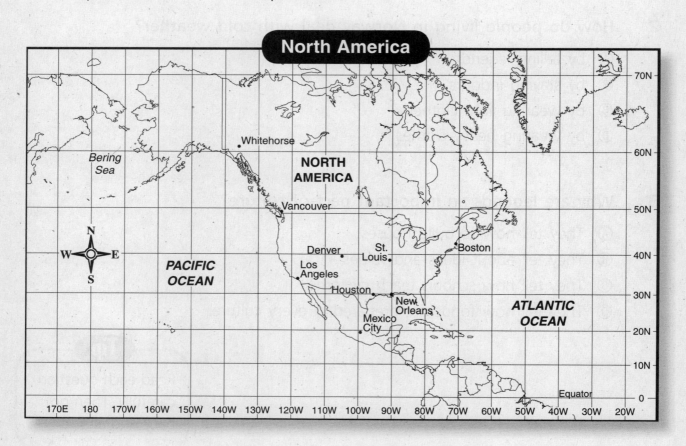

North America

S1 What body of water borders the west coast of most of North America?

Ⓐ Bering Sea

Ⓑ Hudson Bay

Ⓒ Pacific Ocean

Ⓓ Atlantic Ocean

Tip

Look for **labels** on the map to identify which regions and bodies of water are represented.

S2 What is the latitude of New Orleans?

Ⓐ 90°W

Ⓑ 30°S

Ⓒ 30°N

Ⓓ 60°E

Tip

Compare the areas on the map to answer the question.

Name _____ Date _____

Directions

Use the map below and what you know to do Numbers 1–2.

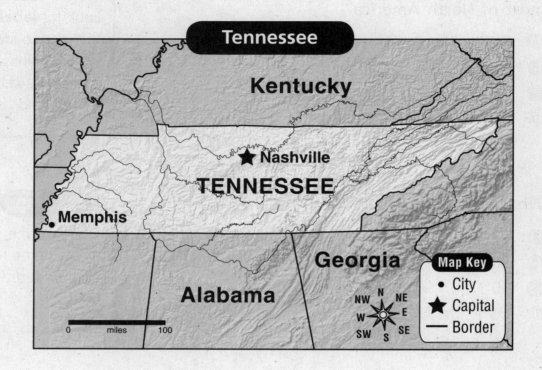

Name _____ Date _____

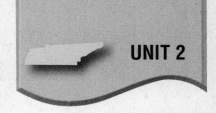

UNIT 2

Reporting Category:	4 Physical Geography
Performance Indicator:	3.3.spi.6 Utilize skills to locate a place using cardinal directions and symbols given an appropriate map with a key.

1 Which state borders Tennessee to the north?

3.3.spi.6

Ⓐ Georgia

Ⓑ Alabama

Ⓒ Kentucky

Ⓓ North Carolina

Reporting Category:	4 Physical Geography
Performance Indicator:	3.3.spi.2 Recognize and use a map key.

2 What is the capital of Tennessee?

3.3.spi.2

Ⓐ Nashville

Ⓑ Knoxville

Ⓒ Memphis

Ⓓ Chattanooga

Get the Most from Nonfiction

Nonfiction is based on facts. When you read nonfiction, your purpose is to learn from those facts. Then be ready to answer questions about them.

Read the passage and strategies on this page. Then look at the questions on the next page.

Using Money

People use money to buy and sell goods and services. Another way to get goods or services is to barter. To barter means to trade. Bartering only works if each person wants something. Money makes trading easier. Bills and coins are small and easy to carry. Money can be used anytime a person wants to buy or sell something.

People work to earn money. They use their income to pay for goods and services. Income is money earned from work. Some people make a budget to see how much income they can spend. It also shows how much they need to save. A budget can also help people decide what to buy.

Many people save the money they don't spend right away. They might save for things such as cars, homes, and school. Saving money is one way to prepare for the future. To save money, people may put it in a bank. When you save money in a bank, your money earns money called interest. The longer you save money at a bank, the more interest your money can earn.

1 Read
Start with the title. As you read, pause and check your understanding.

2 Find
Locate main ideas. Usually, the first sentence in each paragraph tells the **main idea** of the paragraph.

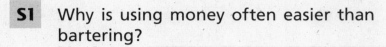

S1 Why is using money often easier than bartering?

3.2.spi.5

  Ⓐ Bartering can only be used for food.

  Ⓑ Bills and coins are difficult to carry.

  Ⓒ People often disagree about what money is worth.

  Ⓓ Money can be used anytime a person wants to buy or sell something.

S2 What is a <u>main</u> difference between using money and bartering?

3.2.spi.5

  Ⓐ Money is only used in the United States.

  Ⓑ Bartering can be used in any store in the world.

  Ⓒ Money is the only way to purchase things today.

  Ⓓ Bartering only works when each person wants something the other has.

41

Directions

Use the passage below and what you know to do Numbers 1–2.

Products, Services, and Trade

Remember that goods are things that people can buy. A <u>producer</u> is someone who makes or sells goods or services to <u>consumers</u>. A consumer is someone who buys goods or services. Producers also provide services. For example, doctors are producers because they provide health services.

People in different regions <u>trade</u> with one another. To trade is to buy and sell goods and services. Tennessee has many resources that producers can use to make and trade products. For example, farmers in Tennessee raise corn to trade with other regions that do not have enough of this crop. Besides corn, Tennessee <u>exports</u> other types of goods. To export means to sell goods or services to people in another country. Tennessee also <u>imports</u> goods and services. To import means to buy goods or services from sellers in other countries.

Name _____ Date _____

Reporting Category:	1 Economics
Performance Indicator:	3.2.spi.3 Distinguish between import and export.

1 Which of the following is an export of Tennessee?

Ⓐ corn

Ⓑ paper

Ⓒ wheat

Ⓓ plastics

Reporting Category:	1 Economics
Performance Indicator:	3.2.spi.4 Differentiate the difference between producer and a consumer using a picture.

2 What is the person who is giving money to buy goods called?

Ⓐ product

Ⓑ producer

Ⓒ consumer

Ⓓ specialist

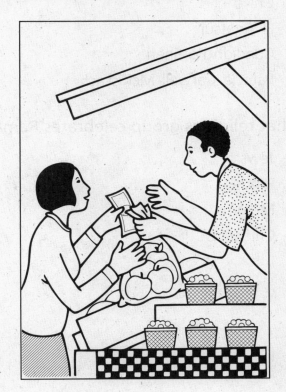

TCAP
PRACTICE
TEST

Reporting Category:	3 Human Geography
Performance Indicator:	3.1.spi.1 Recognize some of the major components of a culture (i.e., language, clothing, food, art, and music).

Directions Use the chart below and what you know to do Number 1.

Artists Around the World		
Artist	**Country**	**Art**
Patricia Carwell McKissack	United States	Children's Books
Candido Portinari	Brazil	Paintings
El Anatsui	Nigeria	Sculptures

1 Which artist is from Brazil?

Ⓐ Chiyo-ni

Ⓑ El Anatsui

Ⓒ Candido Portinari

Ⓓ Patricia Carwell McKissack

2 What religious group celebrates Ramadan?

Ⓐ Jews

Ⓑ Hindus

Ⓒ Muslims

Ⓓ Christians

Name _____ Date _____

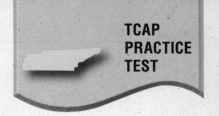
Reporting Category:	4 Physical Geography
Performance Indicator:	3.3.spi.4 Use absolute and relative locations to identify places on a map (i.e., north, south, east, west, borders, lines of longitude and latitude, the equator, the north and south poles).

Directions Use the map below and what you know to do Numbers 3–4.

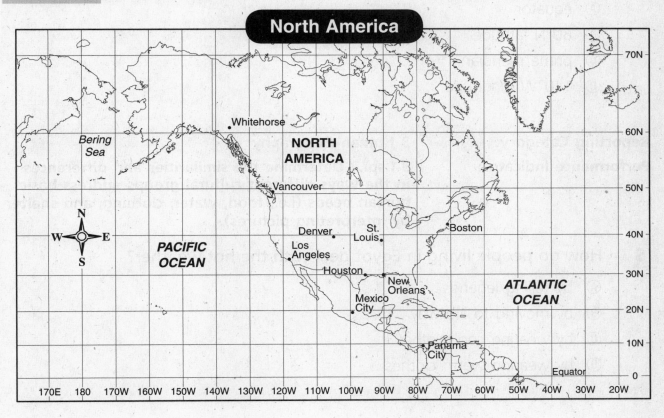

North America

3 What is the latitude and longitude of New Orleans?

Ⓐ about 30°N, 90°W

Ⓑ about 60°N, 30°W

Ⓒ about 30°N, 30°W

Ⓓ about 30°N, 60°W

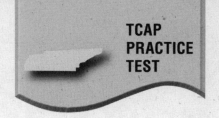

Reporting Category:	4 Physical Geography
Performance Indicator:	3.3.spi.4 Use absolute and relative locations to identify places on a map (i.e., north, south, east, west, borders, lines of longitude and latitude, the equator, the north and south poles).

4 Which line is Panama City closest to?

Ⓐ equator

Ⓑ 60°N latitude

Ⓒ prime meridian

Ⓓ 140°W longitude

Reporting Category:	3 Human Geography
Performance Indicator:	3.1.spi.2 Determine the similarities and differences in the ways different cultural groups address basic human needs (i.e., food, water, clothing, and shelter by interpreting pictures).

5 How do people living in Egypt deal with the hot weather?

Ⓐ by telling legends

Ⓑ by moving to Norway

Ⓒ by wearing cool clothes

Ⓓ by wearing warm clothes

Reporting Category:	4 Physical Geography
Performance Indicator:	3.3.spi.7 Determine the climate of a specific region of the world using a map.

Directions Use the map below and what you know to do Numbers 6–7.

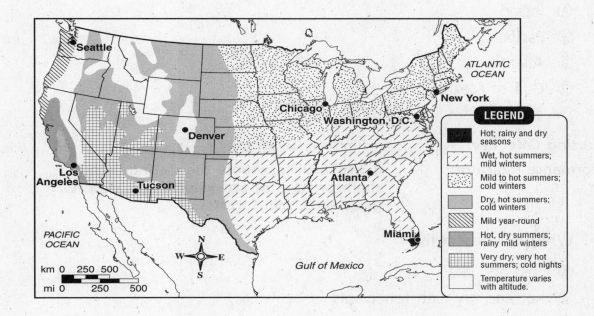

6 What is the climate of the city of Los Angeles?

3.3.spi.7

Ⓐ mild year-round

Ⓑ cold year-round

Ⓒ hot and wet all year

Ⓓ hot, rainy, and dry seasons

Reporting Category:	4 Physical Geography
Performance Indicator:	3.3.spi.1 Identify the major physical components of the world (i.e., oceans, equator, continents, and hemispheres).

7 Which ocean is east of Washington, D.C.?

3.3.spi.1

Ⓐ Indian

Ⓑ Pacific

Ⓒ Atlantic

Ⓓ Gulf of Mexico

Reporting Category:	4 Physical Geography
Performance Indicator:	3.3.spi.8 Differentiate the distinguishing characteristics of ecosystems (i.e., deserts, grasslands, rain forests).

8 What is a desert like?

3.3.spi.8

Ⓐ cold and wet

Ⓑ hot and dry with few plants

Ⓒ hot and wet with tall, thick trees

Ⓓ dry and covered with different grasses

48

Reporting Category:	4 Physical Geography
Performance Indicator:	3.3.spi.9 Recognize the identifying characteristics of certain geographic features (i.e., peninsula, islands, continents, mountains, rivers, deserts, oceans, and forests).

9 Which landform is an area of land surrounded by water on three sides?

Ⓐ delta

Ⓑ island

Ⓒ plateau

Ⓓ peninsula

Reporting Category:	4 Physical Geography
Performance Indicator:	3.3.spi.5 Identify basic components of Earth's systems (i.e., landforms, water, climate, and weather).

10 What is the definition of climate?

Ⓐ a place high in the mountains

Ⓑ weather of a place over a long time

Ⓒ regions that have the same landforms

Ⓓ the time it takes Earth to orbit the Sun

Name _____ Date _____

Reporting Category:	**4 Physical Geography**
Performance Indicator:	**3.3.spi.1 Identify the major physical components of the world (i.e., oceans, equator, continents, and hemispheres).**

Directions Use the map below and what you know to do Numbers 11–12.

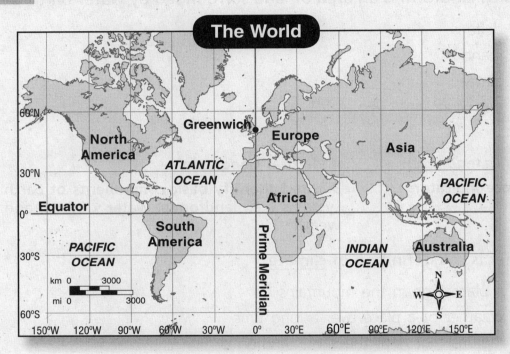

11 Through which two continents does the prime meridian pass?

Ⓐ Asia and Europe

Ⓑ Europe and Africa

Ⓒ Asia and Australia

Ⓓ North America and South America

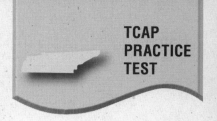

Reporting Category:	4 Physical Geography
Performance Indicator:	3.3.spi.1 Identify the major physical components of the world (i.e., oceans, equator, continents, and hemispheres).

12 Through which two of the following continents does the equator pass?

- Ⓐ Asia and Europe
- Ⓑ Asia and Australia
- Ⓒ Europe and Africa
- Ⓓ Africa and South America

Reporting Category:	4 Physical Geography
Performance Indicator:	3.3.spi.8 Differentiate the distinguishing characteristics of ecosystems (i.e., deserts, grasslands, rain forests).

13 What is an ecosystem?

- Ⓐ a region that is hot and dry with few trees
- Ⓑ the weather in a specific place over a long time
- Ⓒ a dry region that is covered by different types of grass
- Ⓓ all the living and nonliving things that interact with each other in a specific place

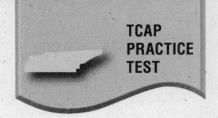

Reporting Category:	3 Human Geography
Performance Indicator:	3.1.spi.1 Recognize some of the major components of a culture (i.e., language, clothing, food, art, and music).

14 Which of the following is a <u>difference</u> among cultures?

Ⓐ saying hello

Ⓑ wearing clothes

Ⓒ living in shelters

Ⓓ eating healthy food

Reporting Category:	4 Physical Geography
Performance Indicator:	3.3.spi.9 Recognize the identifying characteristics of certain geographic features (i.e., peninsula, islands, continents, mountains, rivers, deserts, oceans, and forests).

15 How is the Appalachian region of eastern Tennessee similar to the western United States?

Ⓐ both border oceans

Ⓑ both are flat and dry

Ⓒ both have mountains and valleys

Ⓓ both are flat with rolling grasslands

Reporting Category:	4 Physical Geography
Performance Indicator:	3.3.spi.4 Use absolute and relative locations to identify places on a map (i.e., north, south, east, west, borders, lines of longitude and latitude, the equator, the north and south poles).

Directions Use the map below and what you know to do Numbers 16–17.

16 Which of the following local sites is the farthest south?

3.3.spi.4

Ⓐ City Hall

Ⓑ Rock 'n' Soul Museum

Ⓒ National Civil Rights Museum

Ⓓ Memphis Cook Convention Center

Reporting Category:	4 Physical Geography
Performance Indicator:	3.3.spi.3 Find a specific location on a school or community map.

17 Which local site is located south of Union Avenue and west of Main Street?

Ⓐ City Hall

Ⓑ Rock 'n' Soul Museum

Ⓒ Center for Southern Folklore

Ⓓ Memphis Cook Convention Center

Reporting Category:	4 Physical Geography
Performance Indicator:	3.3.spi.5 Identify basic components of Earth's systems (i.e., landforms, water, climate, and weather).

18 What is erosion?

Ⓐ the weather of a place over a long time

Ⓑ an imaginary line that runs around Earth

Ⓒ the wearing away of land by wind and water

Ⓓ what the air is like at a certain place and time

Name _____ Date _____

Reporting Category:	3 Human Geography
Performance Indicator:	3.1.spi.3 Differentiate the cultural population distribution in the United States using a bar graph.

Directions Use the graph below and what you know to do Numbers 19–20.

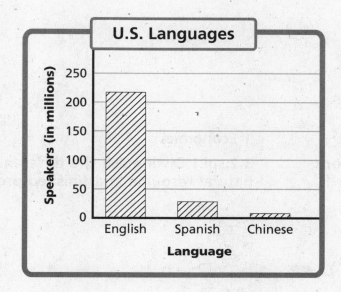

19 What is the second most spoken language in the United States?

Ⓐ French

Ⓑ English

Ⓒ Spanish

Ⓓ Chinese

20 How many people in the United States speak Chinese?

Ⓐ about 2 million

Ⓑ about 50 million

Ⓒ about 100 million

Ⓓ about 200 million

Reporting Category:	4 Physical Geography
Performance Indicator:	3.3.spi.5 Identify basic components of Earth's systems (i.e., landforms, water, climate, and weather).

21 A rain forest and a desert are both examples of

- Ⓐ weather.
- Ⓑ climates.
- Ⓒ landforms.
- Ⓓ ecosystems.

Reporting Category:	1 Economics
Performance Indicator:	3.2.spi.1 Distinguish the differences between a natural resource and finished product.

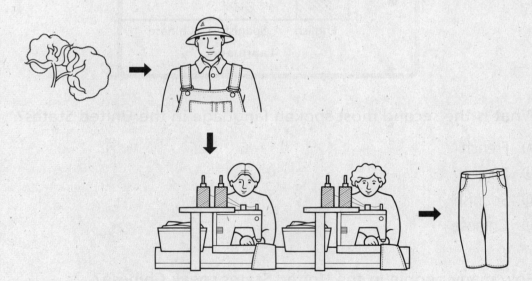

22 Which of the above is a natural resource?

- Ⓐ cotton
- Ⓑ farmer
- Ⓒ blue jeans
- Ⓓ assembly line

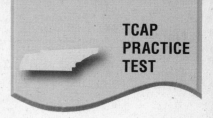

Reporting Category:	1 Economics
Performance Indicator:	3.2.spi.5 Differentiate between money and barter economies.

23 What is barter?

Ⓐ giving something away

Ⓑ getting something for free

Ⓒ buying something with money

Ⓓ trading one product for another

Reporting Category:	4 Physical Geography
Performance Indicator:	3.3.spi.5 Identify basic components of Earth's systems (i.e., landforms, water, climate, and weather).

24 What is deposition?

Ⓐ the weather of a place over a time

Ⓑ what the air is like at a certain time in a certain place

Ⓒ the process by which water breaks down dirt and rock

Ⓓ the process in which water carries dirt from one place and leaves it in another

Reporting Category:	1 Economics
Performance Indicator:	3.2.spi.2 Interpret a map showing agricultural and industrial areas.

Directions Use the map below and what you know to do Numbers 25–26.

25 Which of the following states is mainly industrial?

3.2.spi.2

Ⓐ Indiana (IN)

Ⓑ Kentucky (KY)

Ⓒ Tennessee (TN)

Ⓓ Connecticut (CT)

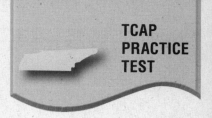

Reporting Category:	1 Economics
Performance Indicator:	3.2.spi.2 Interpret a map showing agricultural and industrial areas.

26 Which state has the most mining activity?

Ⓐ Illinois (IL)

Ⓑ Maine(ME)

Ⓒ Tennessee (TN)

Ⓓ Mississippi (MS)

Reporting Category:	4 Physical Geography
Performance Indicator:	3.3.spi.8 Differentiate the distinguishing characteristics of ecosystems (i.e., deserts, grasslands, rain forests).

27 In which very dry ecosystem do animals hide underground from the heat?

Ⓐ deserts

Ⓑ swamps

Ⓒ grasslands

Ⓓ rain forests

Reporting Category:	1 Economics
Performance Indicator:	3.2.spi.5 Differentiate between money and barter economies.

28 Which of the following is <u>not</u> an example of a barter system?

Ⓐ paying money for a bike

Ⓑ swapping a toy for a book

Ⓒ mowing the yard for candy

Ⓓ trading an apple for an orange

Reporting Category:	1 Economics
Performance Indicator:	3.2.spi.4 Differentiate the difference between producer and a consumer using a picture.

29 What is the person who is receiving money for selling goods called?

Ⓐ product

Ⓑ producer

Ⓒ consumer

Ⓓ specialist

Reporting Category:	1 Economics
Performance Indicator:	3.2.spi.3 Distinguish between import and export.

Directions Use the graph below and what you know to do Numbers 30–31.

Imports and Exports	
Imports from China	**Exports from the United States**
Toys and Sporting Goods	Medical Supplies
Shoes	Aircraft
Clothing	Cars and Trucks

30 Which product does the United States import from China?

Ⓐ oil

Ⓑ toys

Ⓒ aircraft

Ⓓ medicine

31 Which product does the United States export to China?

Ⓐ toys

Ⓑ shoes

Ⓒ aircraft

Ⓓ clothing

Name _____ Date _____

Reporting Category:	1 Economics
Performance Indicator:	3.6.spi.1 Classify needs and wants using pictures of common items (i.e., food, cleaning products, clothes, candy, makeup).

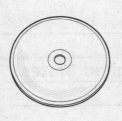  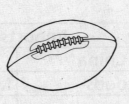 

   A   B   C   D

32 Which of the above pictures is an example of a need?

Ⓐ CD

Ⓑ food

Ⓒ football

Ⓓ trampoline

Reporting Category:	1 Economics
Performance Indicator:	3.2.spi.1 Distinguish the differences between a natural resource and finished product.

33 Which of the following is a finished product?

Ⓐ car

Ⓑ tree

Ⓒ coal

Ⓓ water

Name _____ Date _____

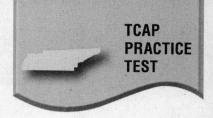

Reporting Category:	1 Economics
Performance Indicator:	3.2.spi.3 Distinguish between import and export.

Directions Use the graph below and what you know to do Numbers 34–35.

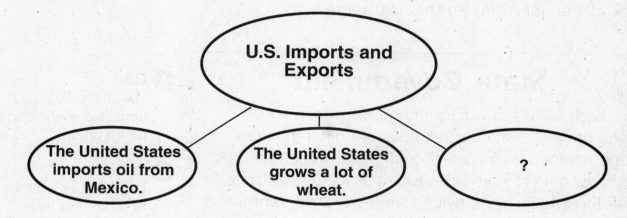

U.S. Imports and Exports

The United States imports oil from Mexico.

The United States grows a lot of wheat.

?

34 Which of these <u>best</u> completes the diagram above?

Ⓐ The United States only trades with Mexico.

Ⓑ The United States needs to import more wheat.

Ⓒ The United States gives away their extra wheat.

Ⓓ The United States exports wheat to other countries.

35 Which of the following is an export of Tennessee?

Ⓐ corn

Ⓑ bananas

Ⓒ pineapples

Ⓓ coconuts

Skills and Strategies

Reading skills help you read well. They also help you do well on tests.

Read the passage and strategies on this page. Then look at the questions on the next page.

State Government

Each state has a constitution, or plan for the government. State constitutions are different from one another. All states, though, have three branches of government that work together to run the state. All three branches provide services to help improve the state and make communities safer.

Lawmakers, who make laws to improve the state and its communities, lead one branch. Your school's rules are like laws. School rules improve the school and keep students safe.

The governor is the head of another branch of government. The governor's main job is to carry out the state laws. The governor of a state can try to stop new laws if he or she disagrees with them.

The court system is also a branch of government. Judges in courts decide whether laws follow the state and national constitutions. Judges also decide whether state laws have been broken. Courts punish people who break laws. People who live in a community must follow its laws.

1 Find
The main idea may appear anywhere in a paragraph.

2 Conclude
Use what you know or what you have read about before to draw conclusions about what the author is trying to say.

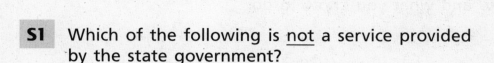

S1 Which of the following is <u>not</u> a service provided by the state government?

3.4.spi.1

Ⓐ making laws to improve the state

Ⓑ getting rid of all taxes on citizens

Ⓒ carrying out new laws to keep citizens safe

Ⓓ deciding whether laws follow the state constitution

Tip

Look at the first paragraph. Find the main idea to answer the question.
Then look for details in the other paragraphs.

S2 In what way do citizens help the government keep the community safe?

3.4.spi.2

Ⓐ They follow the laws of the community.

Ⓑ They don't follow laws they don't agree with.

Ⓒ They have parties for the judges and lawmakers.

Ⓓ They decide whether a law follows the constitution.

Tip

What conclusion can you draw about citizens and the government?

Directions

Use the passage below and what you know to do
Numbers 1–2.

Citizens Make a Difference

Good citizens work together to make their
communities better places to live. There are many
ways you can be a good citizen. Some people help
by working without pay as volunteers. For example,
volunteers in Tennessee helped to build houses in
their state.

United States citizens have many rights, or
freedoms. It is the government's job to protect these
rights. One right that United States citizens have is
the freedom to practice any religion they like or to
practice no religion at all. Another right is freedom
of assembly. This means citizens can meet whenever
they like.

Citizens also have responsibilities. A responsibility
is something you should do for the common good
of your community, state, or nation. Obeying laws
is an important responsibility. Voting is both a right
and a responsibility. Citizens vote to choose leaders
and change laws.

Name _____ Date _____

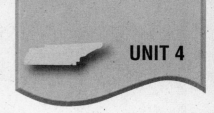

UNIT 4

Reporting Category:	2 Governance and Civics
Performance Indicator:	3.4.spi.2 Determine the representative acts of a good citizen (i.e. obeying speed limit, not littering, walking within the crosswalk).

1 Which <u>best</u> describes a volunteer?

3.4.spi.2

Ⓐ an important responsibility

Ⓑ a person from another country

Ⓒ a person who chooses to work for free

Ⓓ someone who refuses to follow the law

2 Which is <u>both</u> a right and a responsibility?

3.4.spi.2

Ⓐ voting

Ⓑ driving a car

Ⓒ obeying laws

Ⓓ building houses

Put It All Together

You have learned skills and strategies for answering many types of questions. These pages summarize the most important skills that will help you on tests.

Read the passage and strategies on this page. Then look at the questions on the next page.

Working for Rights

Many brave people from Tennessee have worked toward achieving equality for all Americans. One of these people was Sue Shelton White. White was a <u>suffragist</u> born in Henderson in 1887. A suffragist is a person who works for people's right to vote. In the early 1900s, women could not vote. In 1920 Tennessee granted women the right to vote. White helped women gain this right.

James Napier was a Tennessean who worked to gain rights for African Americans. Napier was born in Nashville in 1845. Because of Napier's efforts as a city councilman, the city hired African American teachers for Nashville's African American schools.

Ida B. Wells was another Tennessean who worked to gain rights for African Americans. Wells moved to Tennessee in the 1880s. One day she was asked to give up her seat on a train to a white man. She refused and was forced to get off the train. This event caused Wells to speak out and write about the unfair treatment of African Americans. The articles appeared in newspapers throughout the North.

1 Find
The main idea of a paragraph is often written in the first sentence.

2 Recognize
Look for helpful details that support the main idea of the passage.

3 Summarize
Think about what you have read. Put the main ideas together in one or two sentences.

S1 How did Ida B. Wells help African Americans in Tennessee?

3.5.spi.3

Ⓐ She ran for governor of Tennessee.

Ⓑ She worked to get women the right to vote.

Ⓒ She helped African Americans get elected to the city council.

Ⓓ She spoke out and wrote about the mistreatment of African Americans.

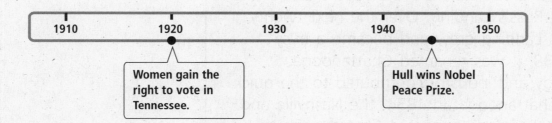

> **Tip**
>
> Look for details in the passage that relate to the question.

S2 Look at the timeline. What year did women gain the right to vote in Tennessee?

3.5.spi.2

Ⓐ 1910

Ⓑ 1920

Ⓒ 1930

Ⓓ 1945

> **Tip**
>
> Look at the timeline and think about the events in the order they occurred.

Name _____ Date _____

Directions
Use the passage below and what you know to do Numbers 1–2.

Chattanooga: The Growth of a City

The city of Chattanooga has a long and rich history. In 1815, a Cherokee named John Ross built a trading post near the Tennessee River where the Cherokee and Creek Indians lived. People called this trading post Ross's Landing. Over the next twenty years, Ross's Landing grew and became a busy town. In 1838, it was renamed Chattanooga.

Technology and industry contributed to the quick growth of Chattanooga. In 1854, the Nashville and Chattanooga Railroad connected Chattanooga to other railroads across the country, bringing new people and businesses to the area. By the 1950s, Chattanooga had many factories making products such as carpet, building materials, and machinery. Unfortunately, the factories polluted the air and water of the city.

Today Chattanooga is the fourth largest city in Tennessee. Factories are still a big part of life in Chattanooga, but efforts by people to clean up the city have helped control the pollution problem. Chattanooga has a very bright future.

UNIT 5

Reporting Category:	3 Human Geography
Performance Indicator:	3.1.spi.1 Recognize some of the major components of a culture (i.e., language, clothing, food, art, and music).

1 How did technology change Chattanooga in the 1800s?

Ⓐ Automobiles made it easier to travel.

Ⓑ The Internet made it easier for people to communicate.

Ⓒ Railroads connected Chattanooga with the rest of the country.

Ⓓ Television brought news and entertainment to people quickly.

Reporting Category:	5 History
Performance Indicator:	3.5.spi.2 Use a timeline to determine the order of a historical sequence of events.

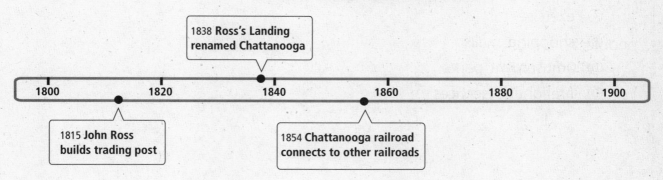

2 What year did the railroad in Chattanooga connect to other railroads?

Ⓐ 1800

Ⓑ 1834

Ⓒ 1854

Ⓓ 1900

Name _____ Date _____

Reporting Category:	2 Governance and Civics
Performance Indicator:	3.4.spi.1 Select from a set of visual representations a service provided by the government (i.e., parks, schools, and libraries).

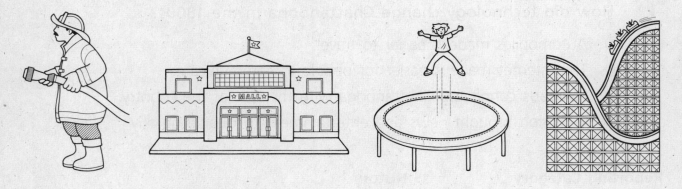

36 Which of the pictured services does the government provide?

3.4.spi.1

Ⓐ exercise

Ⓑ shopping malls

Ⓒ amusement parks

Ⓓ firefighting services

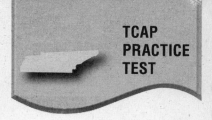

Reporting Category:	1 Economics
Performance Indicator:	3.2.spi.3 Distinguish between import and export.

37 What is an import?

Ⓐ using money to buy a good

Ⓑ trading one good for another

Ⓒ goods bought from other countries

Ⓓ goods bought from the United States

38 What is an export?

Ⓐ a place for airplanes

Ⓑ a place for ships to dock

Ⓒ goods sold to another country

Ⓓ goods bought by the United States

Name _____ Date _____

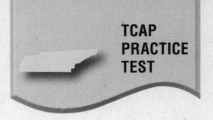

Reporting Category:	2 Governance and Civics
Performance Indicator:	3.4.spi.2 Determine the representative acts of a good citizen (i.e., obeying speed limit, not littering, walking within the crosswalk).

Directions Use the chart below and what you know to do Numbers 39–40.

Rights	Responsibilities
Freedom of religion	Vote for leaders
Freedom on speech	Obey or change laws
Freedom of press	Serve on a jury
Freedom to own property	Respect other people's rights
Freedom to vote for leaders	Speak truthfully

39 Which of the following is a responsibility of a good citizen?

Ⓐ speak truthfully

Ⓑ freedom of the press

Ⓒ freedom to own property

Ⓓ avoid helping other people

40 Which of the following is both a right and a responsibility?

Ⓐ freedom of press

Ⓑ freedom of speech

Ⓒ freedom to own property

Ⓓ freedom to vote for leaders

Name _____ Date _____

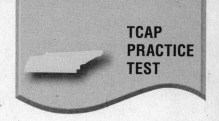

Reporting Category:	3 Human Geography
Performance Indicator:	3.1.spi.4 Interpret a chart or map identifying major cultural groups of the world.

Directions Use the chart below and what you know to do Number 41.

Country and Flag	Type of Government	Leader
United States	**Representative Democracy** Citizens vote for officials to speak for them.	**President** Elected by U.S. citizens
Belize	**Parliamentary Democracy** Lawmakers choose leaders from a political party elected by citizens.	**Prime Minister** Chosen by Belize's lawmakers
Sweden	**Constitutional Monarchy** A ruler, such as a king or queen, lead the country, guided by the country's constitution.	**King or Queen** Power passed down through family

41 How are leaders of Sweden chosen?

3.1.spi.4

Ⓐ Leaders are elected by citizens.

Ⓑ Leaders are chosen by lawmakers.

Ⓒ Leaders are chosen by Parliament.

Ⓓ Power is passed down through a family.

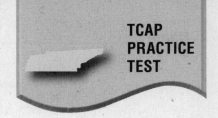

Reporting Category:	2 Governance and Civics
Performance Indicator:	3.4.spi.2 Determine the representative acts of a good citizen (i.e., obeying speed limit, not littering, walking within the crosswalk).

42 Which of the following is <u>not</u> something a good citizen would do?

Ⓐ vote

Ⓑ litter

Ⓒ obey speed limits

Ⓓ walk within crosswalks

43 What is one responsibility of citizens?

Ⓐ obey the laws of the community

Ⓑ choose the community's firefighters

Ⓒ decide which rules they want to follow

Ⓓ say what people can grow their gardens

Reporting Category:	2 Governance and Civics
Performance Indicator:	3.4.spi.2 Determine the representative acts of a good citizen (i.e., obeying speed limit, not littering, walking within the crosswalk).

44 In what way do citizens help keep their communities clean?

- Ⓐ They play in parks and go to school.
- Ⓑ They pick up litter in community parks.
- Ⓒ They disobey laws that they do not agree with.
- Ⓓ They spend time with their families on holidays.

Reporting Category:	3 Human Geography
Performance Indicator:	3.6.spi.3 Recognize major global concerns (i.e., pollution, conservation of natural resources, global warming, destruction of rain forest).

45 What is one solution communities can follow to conserve resources?

- Ⓐ only eat vegetables
- Ⓑ make it illegal to use oil
- Ⓒ only use energy from dams
- Ⓓ recycle paper, plastic, and glass

TCAP Test Practice
77

Reporting Category:	2 Governance and Civics
Performance Indicator:	3.4.spi.2 Determine the representative acts of a good citizen (i.e., obeying speed limit, not littering, walking within the crosswalk).

46 What do good citizens do in a community?

3.4.spi.2

  Ⓐ have parties

  Ⓑ work without pay

  Ⓒ build their own houses

  Ⓓ follow civic responsibilities

47 What does a volunteer do?

3.4.spi.2

  Ⓐ work for money

  Ⓑ does no work at all

  Ⓒ works freely without pay

  Ⓓ doesn't like to do work for others

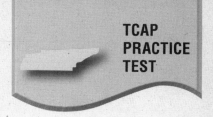

Reporting Category:	3 Human Geography
Performance Indicator:	3.6.spi.3 Recognize major global concerns (i.e., pollution, conservation of natural resources, global warming, destruction of rain forest).

48   What is a role of the Tennessee Department of Environment and Conservation?

3.6.spi.3

Ⓐ build roads

Ⓑ fight pollution

Ⓒ elect the governor

Ⓓ the general assembly

Reporting Category:	5 History
Performance Indicator:	3.5.spi.1 Label historical events as past, present, and future.

49   Which of the following was a Tennessee suffragist of the past?

3.5.spi.1

Ⓐ Robert Scalia

Ⓑ Harriet Tubman

Ⓒ Abraham Lincoln

Ⓓ Sue Shelton White

Reporting Category:	3 Human Geography
Performance Indicator:	3.6.spi.3 Recognize major global concerns (i.e., pollution, conservation of natural resources, global warming, destruction of rain forest).

50 How does public policy help fight pollution?

Ⓐ by hiding trash out of sight

Ⓑ by forcing people to vote on pollution

Ⓒ by creating programs to fight pollution

Ⓓ Public policy cannot help fight pollution.

Reporting Category:	2 Governance and Civics
Performance Indicator:	3.4.spi.2 Determine the representative acts of a good citizen (i.e., obeying speed limit, not littering, walking within the crosswalk).

51 What is one reason we have laws?

Ⓐ to keep a city's population small

Ⓑ to keep people away from suburbs

Ⓒ to make sure people treat each other fairly

Ⓓ to make sure everybody has the same size house

Reporting Category:	4 Physical Geography
Performance Indicator:	3.3.spi.6 Utilize skills to locate a place using cardinal directions and symbols given an appropriate map with a key.

Directions Use the map below and what you know to do Numbers 52–53.

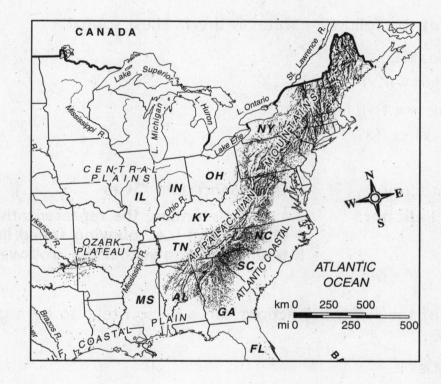

52 Using the map's scale, about how far is Tennessee's western border from the east coast?

3.3.spi.6

Ⓐ 100 miles

Ⓑ 250 miles

Ⓒ 500 miles

Ⓓ 800 miles

Reporting Category:	4 Physical Geography
Performance Indicator:	3.3.spi.4 Use absolute and relative locations to identify places on a map (i.e., north, south, east, west, borders, lines of longitude and latitude, the equator, the north and south poles).

53 Which of the following states is the farthest south?

3.3.spi.4

Ⓐ Florida (FL)

Ⓑ Kentucky (KY)

Ⓒ Tennessee (TN)

Ⓓ Mississippi (MS)

Reporting Category:	2 Governance and Civics
Performance Indicator:	3.4.spi.2 Determine the representative acts of a good citizen (i.e., obeying speed limit, not littering, walking within the crosswalk).

54 Which of the following actions can a person take to be a good citizen?

3.4.spi.2

Ⓐ recycle

Ⓑ buy candy

Ⓒ move away

Ⓓ see a movie

| Reporting Category: | 5 History |
| Performance Indicator: | 3.5.spi.1 Label historical events as past, present, and future. |

55 What movement did African American leaders start in the 1950s and 1960s?

Ⓐ antiwar movement

Ⓑ suffrage movement

Ⓒ civil rights movement

Ⓓ elderly rights movement

Directions Use the chart below and what you know to do Number 56.

Tennessee Hero	Accomplishment	Born
Cordell Hull	Helped form the United Nations	1871
Nancy Ward	Worked for peace between the Cherokee and the settlers	1738
Austin Peay	Governor who built roads and schools	1876

56 What year was Governor Austin Peay born?

Ⓐ 1738

Ⓑ 1876

Ⓒ 1787

Ⓓ 1870

Reporting Category:	5 History
Performance Indicator:	3.5.spi.1 Label historical events as past, present, and future.

57 In the mid-1700s, which Tennessean worked to settle disputes between the Cherokee and settlers?

Ⓐ Nancy Ward

Ⓑ Austin Peay

Ⓒ Cordell Hull

Ⓓ Davy Crockett

58 From 1952 to 1993, how did Cesar Chavez help farm workers?

Ⓐ He spoke out for their rights.

Ⓑ He helped workers fight pollution.

Ⓒ He brought workers new technology.

Ⓓ He worked to get farm workers the right to vote.

Reporting Category:	**5 History**
Performance Indicator:	**3.5.spi.2 Use a timeline to determine the order of a historical sequence of events.**

Directions Use the timeline below and what you know to do Numbers 59–60.

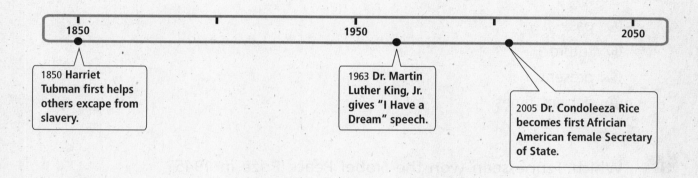

1850 **Harriet Tubman first helps others excape from slavery.**

1963 **Dr. Martin Luther King, Jr. gives "I Have a Dream" speech.**

2005 **Dr. Condoleeza Rice becomes first Africian American female Secretary of State.**

59 What year did Martin Luther King, Jr. give his "I Have a Dream" speech?

3.5.spi.2

Ⓐ 1857

Ⓑ 1950

Ⓒ 1963

Ⓓ 2005

TCAP Test Practice
85

Reporting Category:	5 History
Performance Indicator:	3.5.spi.1 Label historical events as past, present and future.

60 In which of the following periods did Harriet Tubman first help others escape from slavery?

Ⓐ past

Ⓑ future

Ⓒ present

Ⓓ ancient times

61 Which Tennessean won the Nobel Peace Prize in 1945?

Ⓐ Cordell Hull

Ⓑ Harriet Tubman

Ⓒ Abraham Lincoln

Ⓓ Franklin D. Roosevelt

Reporting Category:	5 History
Performance Indicator:	3.5.spi.1 Label historical events as past, present and future.

62 What did Abraham Lincoln do to help end slavery in 1863?

ⓐ He ended the Civil War.

ⓑ He started the Revolutionary War.

ⓒ He bought Louisiana from France.

ⓓ He issued the Emancipation Proclamation.

Reporting Category:	3 Human Geography
Performance Indicator:	3.1.spi.1 Recognize some of the major components of a culture (i.e. language, clothing, food, art, and music).

63 Which of the following was an important part of Athens' culture?

ⓐ advertising

ⓑ the military

ⓒ art and stories

ⓓ new technology

Reporting Category:	5 Governance and Civics
Performance Indicator:	3.6.spi.2 Distinguish between conflict and cooperation within group interactions as represented by pictures.

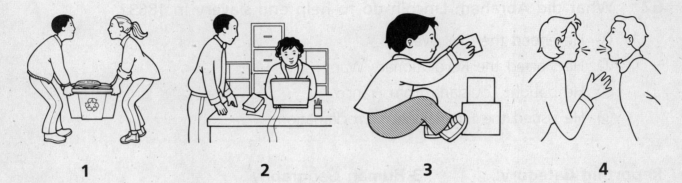

1   **2**   **3**   **4**

64 Which of the above pictures shows an example of cooperation?

Ⓐ 1

Ⓑ 2

Ⓒ 3

Ⓓ 4

65 Which of the above pictures shows an example of conflict?

Ⓐ 1

Ⓑ 2

Ⓒ 3

Ⓓ 4

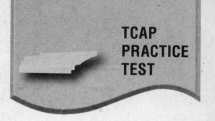

Reporting Category:	5 History
Performance Indicator:	3.5.spi.2 Use a timeline to determine the order of a historical sequence of events.

Directions Use the timeline below and what you know to do Numbers 66–69.

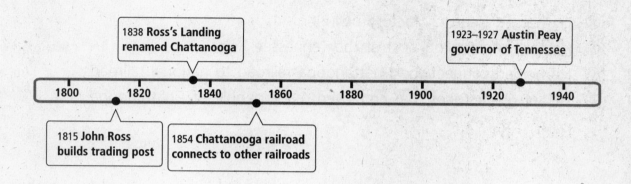

66 What year was Ross's Landing renamed Chattanooga?

3.5:spi.2

Ⓐ 1800

Ⓑ 1834

Ⓒ 1838

Ⓓ 1854

Name _____ Date _____

TCAP
PRACTICE
TEST

Reporting Category:	5 History
Performance Indicator:	3.5.spi.2 Use a timeline to determine the order of a historical sequence of events.

67 How did John Ross help shape Chattanooga?

Ⓐ He helped clean up factory pollution.

Ⓑ He set up a trading post at the Tennessee River.

Ⓒ He helped connect the Chattanooga railroad to national railroads.

Ⓓ He set up factories that employed many people of Chattanooga.

68 According to the timeline, about how many decades passed between Ross building a trading post and Chattanooga being named?

Ⓐ about 2 decades

Ⓑ about 3 decades

Ⓒ about 4 decades

Ⓓ about 5 decades

Reporting Category:	5 History
Performance Indicator:	3.5.spi.1 Label historical events as past, present and future.

69 What years was Austin Peay governor of Tennessee?
3.5.spi.1

Ⓐ 1776–1778

Ⓑ 1882–1886

Ⓒ 1923–1927

Ⓓ 1986–1999

Reporting Category:	3 Human Geography
Performance Indicator:	3.1.spi.1 Recognize some of the major components of a culture (i.e. language, clothing, food, art, and music).

70 How did technology change Chattanooga in the 1800s?
3.1.spi.1

Ⓐ Automobiles made it easier to travel.

Ⓑ The Internet made it easier for people to communicate.

Ⓒ Railroads connected Chattanooga with the rest of the country.

Ⓓ Television brought news and entertainment to people quickly.

TCAP Practice Test — Part 1

1. Ⓐ Ⓑ Ⓒ Ⓓ
2. Ⓐ Ⓑ Ⓒ Ⓓ
3. Ⓐ Ⓑ Ⓒ Ⓓ
4. Ⓐ Ⓑ Ⓒ Ⓓ
5. Ⓐ Ⓑ Ⓒ Ⓓ
6. Ⓐ Ⓑ Ⓒ Ⓓ
7. Ⓐ Ⓑ Ⓒ Ⓓ
8. Ⓐ Ⓑ Ⓒ Ⓓ
9. Ⓐ Ⓑ Ⓒ Ⓓ
10. Ⓐ Ⓑ Ⓒ Ⓓ
11. Ⓐ Ⓑ Ⓒ Ⓓ
12. Ⓐ Ⓑ Ⓒ Ⓓ
13. Ⓐ Ⓑ Ⓒ Ⓓ
14. Ⓐ Ⓑ Ⓒ Ⓓ
15. Ⓐ Ⓑ Ⓒ Ⓓ
16. Ⓐ Ⓑ Ⓒ Ⓓ
17. Ⓐ Ⓑ Ⓒ Ⓓ
18. Ⓐ Ⓑ Ⓒ Ⓓ

19. Ⓐ Ⓑ Ⓒ Ⓓ
20. Ⓐ Ⓑ Ⓒ Ⓓ
21. Ⓐ Ⓑ Ⓒ Ⓓ
22. Ⓐ Ⓑ Ⓒ Ⓓ
23. Ⓐ Ⓑ Ⓒ Ⓓ
24. Ⓐ Ⓑ Ⓒ Ⓓ
25. Ⓐ Ⓑ Ⓒ Ⓓ
26. Ⓐ Ⓑ Ⓒ Ⓓ
27. Ⓐ Ⓑ Ⓒ Ⓓ
28. Ⓐ Ⓑ Ⓒ Ⓓ
29. Ⓐ Ⓑ Ⓒ Ⓓ
30. Ⓐ Ⓑ Ⓒ Ⓓ
31. Ⓐ Ⓑ Ⓒ Ⓓ
32. Ⓐ Ⓑ Ⓒ Ⓓ
33. Ⓐ Ⓑ Ⓒ Ⓓ
34. Ⓐ Ⓑ Ⓒ Ⓓ
35. Ⓐ Ⓑ Ⓒ Ⓓ

TCAP Practice Test — Part 2

36. Ⓐ Ⓑ Ⓒ Ⓓ
37. Ⓐ Ⓑ Ⓒ Ⓓ
38. Ⓐ Ⓑ Ⓒ Ⓓ
39. Ⓐ Ⓑ Ⓒ Ⓓ
40. Ⓐ Ⓑ Ⓒ Ⓓ
41. Ⓐ Ⓑ Ⓒ Ⓓ
42. Ⓐ Ⓑ Ⓒ Ⓓ
43. Ⓐ Ⓑ Ⓒ Ⓓ
44. Ⓐ Ⓑ Ⓒ Ⓓ
45. Ⓐ Ⓑ Ⓒ Ⓓ
46. Ⓐ Ⓑ Ⓒ Ⓓ
47. Ⓐ Ⓑ Ⓒ Ⓓ
48. Ⓐ Ⓑ Ⓒ Ⓓ
49. Ⓐ Ⓑ Ⓒ Ⓓ
50. Ⓐ Ⓑ Ⓒ Ⓓ
51. Ⓐ Ⓑ Ⓒ Ⓓ
52. Ⓐ Ⓑ Ⓒ Ⓓ
53. Ⓐ Ⓑ Ⓒ Ⓓ

54. Ⓐ Ⓑ Ⓒ Ⓓ
55. Ⓐ Ⓑ Ⓒ Ⓓ
56. Ⓐ Ⓑ Ⓒ Ⓓ
57. Ⓐ Ⓑ Ⓒ Ⓓ
58. Ⓐ Ⓑ Ⓒ Ⓓ
59. Ⓐ Ⓑ Ⓒ Ⓓ
60. Ⓐ Ⓑ Ⓒ Ⓓ
61. Ⓐ Ⓑ Ⓒ Ⓓ
62. Ⓐ Ⓑ Ⓒ Ⓓ
63. Ⓐ Ⓑ Ⓒ Ⓓ
64. Ⓐ Ⓑ Ⓒ Ⓓ
65. Ⓐ Ⓑ Ⓒ Ⓓ
66. Ⓐ Ⓑ Ⓒ Ⓓ
67. Ⓐ Ⓑ Ⓒ Ⓓ
68. Ⓐ Ⓑ Ⓒ Ⓓ
69. Ⓐ Ⓑ Ⓒ Ⓓ
70. Ⓐ Ⓑ Ⓒ Ⓓ